Danny's Special Tree

written and photographed
by
Mia Coulton

All trees are special.

This is a very special tree.

This is Danny's tree.

3

It is a sunny day.

Danny is resting under his big

red maple tree.

He is not hot because his tree

gives him shade.

Danny is thinking about all the things

we get from trees.

He thinks about the paper he uses
to draw pictures. The paper is made
from   trees.

He thinks about the maple syrup that is on top of his Saturday morning pancakes. The maple syrup is made from sap that comes from the *sugar maple* tree.

Danny looks up. He sees a mama bird feeding her baby birds. Her nest is in the birdhouse which is made from wood. Wood is made from trees.

The birdhouse is hanging from a branch of the tree. Danny's tree is shelter for the bird family. His tree is also shelter for many animals and insects.

A leaf from Danny's tree falls to the ground. Danny looks at the leaf.

The leaves on trees are special too.
They make food for trees.

The leaves pull water up from the ground by way of the roots. Then they take a gas called carbon dioxide from the air.

Leaves take energy from the sun to mix the water and the carbon dioxide together. This makes tree food.

When leaves make their food, they also make a gas called oxygen. The leaves do not need all the oxygen they make, so they put what they do not use into the air for animals, like Danny, and people to breathe.

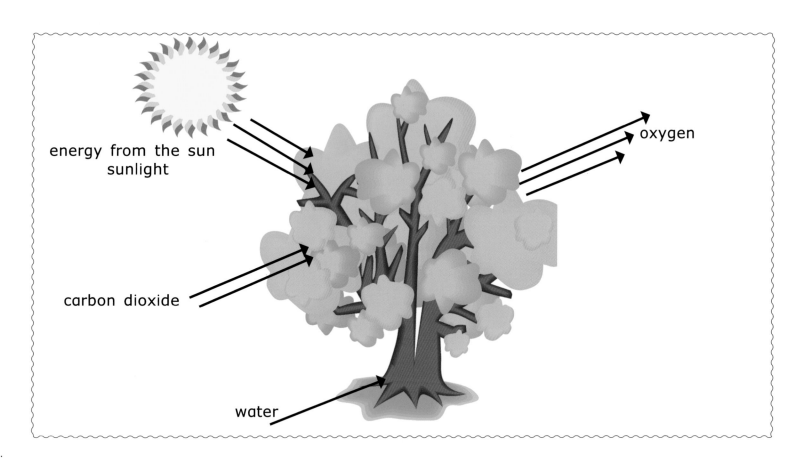

The making of food by plants and trees is called *photosynthesis*.

Danny loves big words like *photosynthesis*.

Danny loves his tree. He loves all trees. Trees are good friends to Danny and the earth. He makes a promise to be a good friend to the trees and the earth.

DANNY'S PROMISE

I promise to reduce, reuse, and recycle to help save our trees and protect the earth.

I will **reduce**.

If I spill my water, I will clean it up with a rag, not a paper towel.

I will reuse.

When I go to the store, I will bring my canvas bag.

I will **recycle**.

I will recycle cardboard boxes and papers.

I will learn more about trees
and other plants.

I will learn more about the earth.

I will ask questions and try to find answers.

LIBRARY   CARD

Maybe I will be a scientist.

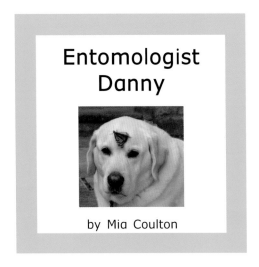

Entomologist
Danny

by Mia Coulton

Botanist
Danny

by Mia Coulton

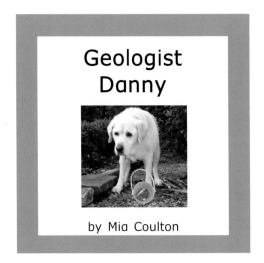

Geologist
Danny

by Mia Coulton